TRANSFORMERS
REVENGE OF THE FALLEN

THE JUNIOR NOVEL

Transformers: Revenge of The Fallen: The Junior Novel

TRANSFORMERS, the logo, and all related characters are trademarks of Hasbro and are used with permission.
© 2009 Hasbro. All Rights Reserved.

© 2009 DreamWorks, LLC and Paramount Pictures Corporation. All Rights Reserved.

HarperCollins®, 🅼®, and HarperEntertainment™ are trademarks of HarperCollins Publishers.

Printed in the United States of America.

www.harpercollinschildrens.com

Library of Congress catalog card number: 2008940050

ISBN 978-0-06-172973-7

09 10 11 12 13   LP/CW/UG   10 9 8 7 6 5 4 3 2

❖

First Edition

TRANSFORMERS
REVENGE OF THE FALLEN

THE JUNIOR NOVEL

Adapted by Dan Jolley

Based on the Screenplay by

Ehren Kruger & Alex Kurtzman

& Roberto Orci

HarperEntertainment

An Imprint of HarperCollinsPublishers

Home.
Ours was once a planet called Cybertron. Until the War brought its destruction and made exiles of us all.

The lone hope for our race lay with the recovery of the AllSpark. All-knowing, all-seeing, it was the keeper of our history. It held the secrets of our kind. But with its destruction, only fragments now remain.

I am Optimus Prime, leader of the Autobots. We take shelter on this Earth in hiding, awaiting the arrival of more Autobot allies. But in our quest to defend the humans, a deeper revelation dawns.

Our worlds have met before.

Thin, wispy clouds touched the tops of distant mountains as dawn began to break.

A group of hunters crept through tall grass, each of them carrying a spear. Their prey—an enormous tiger—lay ahead of them, unaware of their presence.

Suddenly a gigantic metal foot slammed down right in front of them. The hunters screamed and scrambled backward, looking up at the enormous metal monster that towered above them. The hunters didn't know that what they saw was a Transformer from the planet Cybertron. They had no idea that the alien's angular, crowned face was the symbol for the group of Transformers known as Decepticons. And they would never know that the Decepticon staring down at them was known as The Fallen.

The men fell to their knees, terrified, as the tiger sprinted away. The Fallen picked up one of the men but soon dropped him in disgust. He seemed repulsed that the hunter was alive. Turning away, The Fallen ignored the men completely and headed for the nearby canyon.

The hunters helped their companion to his feet and followed the gigantic metal creature. What they saw at the canyon's edge amazed them. Dozens more of the enormous beings moved about on the canyon floor. From the center of the canyon rose a gleaming metal spire, thousands of times higher than any structure the men had ever seen.

The night air filled with the screech of tires and the sound of men's voices shouting.

The Chinese police cordoned off one of the older sections of the city; they were reasonably sure everyone had been evacuated.

Closer to the water's edge, next to a huge building lined on one side with loading docks, a black eighteen-wheeler rumbled by, moving fast. Its rear door dropped open, and a group of Hummers raced out, each one filled with men in full hazmat suits. The men carried high-tech weaponry and state-of-the-art search-and-seek equipment. Blinking sensors and small, bright computer screens filled the interior of each vehicle with an eerie glow.

Nearby, at a huge industrial steelyard, Blackhawk helicopters dropped out of the sky and began circling, their powerful search beams lancing through the night sky. Other helicopters—Cobra gunships—hovered nearby, providing backup to the Blackhawks if they needed it.

On the ground below, the Hummers skidded to a stop and their passengers spilled out. One of the men checked a sensor unit, waited to confirm a certain reading, and then signaled an *okay* to the rest of the group. The men all began pulling off their hazmat suits, revealing the military uniforms of both the United States and Great Britain.

In the cargo hold of one of the circling Blackhawks, Major William Lennox and Master Sergeant Ray Epps eyeballed the rest of the passengers—all British troops—as Lennox spoke into his headset.

Lennox and Epps had both faced this kind of threat before; in fact, they had played crucial roles in helping the Autobots defeat Megatron and the rest of the Decepticons when the aliens had first arrived on Earth. Now, many months later, both men were back in the thick of it.

"All right, guys," Lennox said. "Six enemy contacts in eight months—we gotta make sure this one does *not* get into the public eye. Keep it tight. Let's rock."

Epps flashed him a grin. "Thought we were rollin' today."

The Blackhawk dipped low and hovered. Lennox, Epps, and the British soldiers jumped out and scattered forward, seeking cover. Epps checked out the area with special night-vision goggles, fitted with an AllSpark detector.

"Lotta interference on this one," Epps said quietly. "Infrared signature's at four bars."

Lennox scowled. "*Four?* You gotta be kidding me."

One of the British soldiers spoke up. "Either it's cloaking its signal—like it did in Rome—or we're getting echoes off those steel stacks."

Lennox activated his headset again. "Tell our four-by-four friend he's clear."

Seconds later, a powerful-looking black pickup truck rolled into the steelyard, with more soldiers riding in the bed. The soldiers leaped off, and the truck changed, thousands upon thousands of mechanical pieces disconnecting, rearranging, and reconnecting. The truck broke apart, rose up on two feet, and came back together in the form of one of the Autobots that Lennox and Epps trusted most: Ironhide.

The huge Autobot locked eyes with Lennox, who nodded in response.

Epps said, "Time to kick some butt and take some names."

Lennox rolled his eyes. "Getting cocky, Epps."

Epps thumbed off the safety on his assault rifle. "We're 'bout to go after some kinda classified alien predator—you want me cocky or scared outta my mind?"

Lennox considered that. "All right, cocky's good. Ironhide, we've got echoes—steel stacks at two o'clock."

Ironhide's head swiveled as he scanned their surroundings. "He's here. . . . He's close. . . ."

"Then let's amplify his pain." Lennox gave Ironhide a signal.

Ironhide said, "Sideswipe, deploy."

Behind them, another eighteen-wheeler had arrived and parked; its rear door dropped open now, and a sleek, ultracool Corvette sped out. The Corvette immediately switched forms, becoming a streamlined Autobot, clearly built for speed even when not on four wheels. Sideswipe drew out a twin pair of swords, ready for action.

An ice cream truck suddenly skidded around a corner and headed toward Ironhide and the soldiers. Ironhide spotted it, sighed, and said, "Twins, just ... try and stay out of trouble, all right? Watch the big boys."

At that instant a huge stack of nearby cement pipes exploded, hurled aside by a gigantic construction vehicle. This new threat immediately switched forms, becoming a colossal two-wheeled engine of destruction that towered forty feet above the soldiers.

The Decepticon, Demolisher, made a break for it, trying to escape. The men opened fire with rockets on the monstrosity, but nothing seemed to stop it as it tore its way out of the steelyard.

Hot on Demolisher's trail, a Decepticon disguised as a European sports car zoomed out of hiding and rushed off down the road after its much larger companion.

The sports car split off from the monster-sized Demolisher, ripping around corners and speeding through tight alleys. The ice cream truck came roaring after it, but the sports car sped through an incredibly narrow path between buildings.

The ice cream truck tried to follow, but it was too wide, and its sides jammed against the brick walls. An ordinary ice cream truck would have been stuck tight, but this one just split in half; the two halves changed into small Autobots and stood up.

One of them chided the other, speaking the Autobots' extraterrestrial language. The second one balled up his fist and punched the first one, knocking him flat.

Sideswipe swept in, fast and low, and slashed one of the Decepticon's legs with a sword, rendering the limb useless. The sports car screamed just as Lennox and the rest of the soldiers came pouring out of the hole it had made in the wall.

"Pin him down!" Lennox shouted.

The Decepticon tried to resist, but Sideswipe was too fast, and a very precise sword stroke to the head put the enemy flat on the ground.

Sparks popped and hissed from its mouth, but it didn't move anymore.

Already a mile away, the giant Demolisher crashed onto a Shanghai freeway, bashing cars aside left and right. It brought one wheel up in the air and started smashing the wheels down, one in front of the other. High overhead, a C-17 cargo plane swooped low and opened its doors—and out dropped a massive blue semitruck with red detailing and yellow flames, plummeting through the air.

Optimus Prime.

Prime switched forms in midair and released three parachutes, each one with the Autobot symbol on it. He guided his descent carefully and landed squarely on Demolisher's neck.

Ironhide, again in truck form, barreled up beside the Decepticon, slid underneath its massive frame, and caught onto the lower wheel.

"Now!" Prime shouted, and he and Ironhide both slammed Demolisher with all their combined strength.

The huge Transformer wobbled and tipped

sideways, crashing to the ground as Prime and Ironhide leaped clear.

Prime slowly, carefully approached the wounded Decepticon. His face had been partially crushed by the impact, so his voice was garbled, but he gasped out the words: "This is not your planet to rule. . . . The Fallen . . . shall rise . . . again. . . ."

Demolisher lapsed into inertness as Prime and Ironhide stood there, puzzled by what the Decepticon had said.

am Witwicky busily packed for college. He was cramming things from his closet into a big cardboard box.

His father Ron's voice drifted up from downstairs. "Let's go, let's go, all hands on deck!"

Sam smiled, taped the heavy box shut, and hauled it downstairs. He almost tripped over his Chihuahua, Mojo. Mojo was chasing the new dog, Frankie, a French bulldog, in circles around the room. Sam carefully set the big box on top of a stack next to the door.

Ron clapped his hands at the dogs. "Mojo! Frankie! Outside, outside!" He gave Sam a stern look. "C'mon, kiddo, we're on a schedule here!"

"Dad, seriously, why're you in such a hurry

to get rid of me? You rented out my room, didn't you?"

"No, I have other plans for your room, and it rhymes with 'home theater.'"

Sam grinned. He would have retorted, but just then his mother Judy burst into the room, sobbing and clutching a pair of white baby shoes.

"Look what I found, your baby booties! I'm losing my baby! C'mere, my bitty booty baby . . . !"

Before Sam could stop her, Judy pulled him into a suffocating hug. Over her shoulder, Sam said to his father, "See? *This* is how you're supposed to react, Dad."

Ron was unmoved. "Yeah. College. My heart bleeds for you."

Through her tears, Judy said, "I want you back here every holiday, even Presidents Day. And Halloween."

Sam stepped back from her. "Mom, they don't let us off for Halloween."

Judy's eyes lit up. "We'll come to you!"

"No, you will not—"

She went on. "We'll dress up in costumes, no one'll recognize us. I'm your mother. . . ."

"My mother, not my smother," Sam said, putting a reassuring hand on her shoulder. "Just drop me off, go do your thing, go to Europe, get a short haircut, I'll see you at graduation. Love you. Send money!"

Ron stepped closer to her as her lower lip trembled. "Judy, let the kid breathe, okay? And there's no *way* you're done packing for a monthlong trip. Chop, chop!"

Judy made it up the first two stairs before her budding smile crumbled. She turned back to Ron. "Oh, Ron . . . we're losing our baby. The only baby we ever had!" Bursting into tears again, she fled up to the second floor.

Ron watched her go, shook his head, and put his arm around Sam's shoulders. "We're both real proud of you, kiddo. First Witwicky ever to go to college. And the *way* you did it! Solid B's to straight A's overnight, nearly perfect SATs, parlayed into an Ivy League school on the East Coast. . . . How you pulled it off is beyond me."

"Thanks, Dad." Sam's forehead wrinkled. "Me, too, actually."

Ron hesitated. "Now . . . you know you're going

to meet a lot of girls out there."

Sam smiled. "And *you* know I'm a one-girl kind of guy, Pop."

Ron nodded but continued. "Look, Mikaela's the greatest, but you gotta give each other room to grow. Be honest about the fact that you'll end up seeing other people. You're no different than any other couple your age—"

Sam chuckled. "Except we discovered an alien race and saved the world together."

"Yeah, yeah, yeah—how long you gonna keep riding on that one thing?"

As if to save Sam from answering his father's question, his cell phone rang. A name flashed up on the LCD screen: *Mikaela.* Sam grinned. "See? She can't get enough of me. I know the odds, Dad. But we're the exception." Sam hit the *talk* button, held the phone up to his father's mouth, and said, "Say, 'Hey, beautiful.'"

Ron rolled his eyes. "Hey, beautiful."

Sam took the phone back and spoke into it. "Whaddaya think? That's what I'm gonna sound like in eighty years."

Several miles away, in her father's motorcycle

shop, a beautiful girl with lustrous, wavy dark hair used her cell phone headset to talk while she worked. As she airbrushed a custom painting onto a bike, Mikaela said, "I'm breaking up with you."

Sam walked back up to his bedroom, unfazed. "Yeah, I don't know—gotta be honest, I'm not hearing a lot of conviction."

"Well, I am," Mikaela said, "and I mean it, so there's no point in me coming to say good-bye."

"Wow, you almost sounded serious that time. Guess what?"

Mikaela set down the airbrush. "You found your future wife on the freshman Facebook page?"

Sam entered his room and took a cigar box from a drawer. Inside it rested a webcam, some mixed CDs, his great-great-grandfather's famous glasses, and a Sector Seven badge. Those last two were mementos of the adventure that Sam and Mikaela had shared.

"No, I'm making you a long-distance relation-ship kit, complete with webcam so we can chat 24/7. All Witwicky, all the time."

Mikaela sat back on her stool. "Cute . . . Can't wait. . . ." She tried not to smile. Sam's charm got to her. It always did.

He said, "You could always come with me, you know."

She sighed. "And you know I need to stay here and help my dad. Just for a while."

"Yeah. You *are* coming over, though, right?"

"Be there in twenty."

Sam hung up the phone and pulled a ragged, torn, charred shirt from the drawer. It was the shirt he had worn when he'd met Bumblebee . . . and been arrested by Sector Seven . . . and fought Megatron, the Decepticon leader, over the AllSpark.

Sam noticed something: a charred ember, stuck in the shirt's material. He touched it. Suddenly his mind filled with thousands and thousands of images, changing in a rapid-fire barrage of information. Strange alien symbols seemed to be burning onto his brain.

The symbols were from the AllSpark!

Sam's hand flew open, and he dropped the ember on the floor. It lay there, its light going out slowly. When it finally darkened completely, Sam picked it up with a handkerchief and dropped it into an empty film canister.

A few minutes later, Mikaela pulled up to the curb on a fast-looking Japanese motorcycle. Sam met her there, kissed her briefly, and handed her the canister. "Keep this hidden, will you? Someplace safe."

She nodded and put the canister in her pocket. "What is it?"

"Maybe nothing. I'm not sure. But right now I've gotta give a friend some bad news. Come with me?"

Together Sam and Mikaela walked into the garage. Bumblebee, Sam's Autobot guardian, crouched there in robot form, his head hunched down so as not to bang into the roof. He tried to speak, but all that came out was a series of electronic whistles and shrieks.

Sympathetic, Mikaela asked, "Still having voice problems?"

Bumblebee nodded sadly. Sam said, "Listen. Bee. Uh . . . about college. I wanted to talk to you about that. . . . "

Abandoning any attempts at real speech, Bumblebee used his radio to play a really upbeat song.

Sam tried to talk, but Bumblebee kept playing the song.

Finally Sam raised his voice. *"I'm not taking you with me!"*

The song shut off, and Bumblebee's blue eyes widened.

Mikaela said, "Uh . . . I'll be outside," and exited the garage.

Sam struggled to keep his voice even. "Look, I meant to tell you a while ago, it's just . . . freshmen aren't allowed to have cars. It's a rule."

Bumblebee looked away, his shoulders slumping. Sam sighed, reached up, and took Bumblebee's face, turning it back toward him. "But you need your freedom, don't you? So you can be with the other Autobots. You have a bigger . . . purpose. Right?"

Bumblebee switched from songs to rapid clips from commercials: "What . . . is . . . *your* . . . purpose . . . Sam?"

Sam stepped back and shrugged. "I don't know. Be normal. Go to college and figure out what I want. And I gotta do that . . . alone."

Bumblebee sighed, a long, lonely sound. A melancholy love song played from his radio.

"Bee, hey, c'mon. It's not like we're never gonna see each other again. . . . You'll always be my first car." Bumblebee nodded sadly. Sam gave him a last look and left the garage.

Outside he found Mikaela waiting for him at the head of the driveway. He stepped behind her and put his arms around her. "You know you're the best thing that ever happened to me," he whispered.

She smiled, but one eyebrow raised a little. "And?"

"And . . . I'd do anything for you."

"*And?*"

"I . . . adore you."

Impatient now: "'Adore'?"

"What? Adore is like the highest form of . . . adoration! It's basically the same as the other word. Anyway, if I say it now, it'll be forced. Besides, you never said the other word, either, so don't get on me about—"

She rolled her eyes. "Because guys always run when you say it first."

"So do girls! Especially girls like *you*. With options. *Lots* of options."

Mikaela turned around to face him. "So, all this—going to college, being the strong and silent type—it's all your elaborate plan to keep me interested?"

Sam grinned. "It can be."

She pouted. "I hate that it's working."

They kissed, and then Sam pulled away and headed for the car, which was waiting at the end of the driveway with his parents in it. "We're gonna make this work," he told her. "I promise."

Two minutes later, as the car rolled away down the street and Mikaela wiped a tear from her eye, a tiny remote-controlled truck peered out from behind the tire of another car parked down the block.

The truck, Wheels, was a Decepticon spy. It watched as Mikaela got on her bike, and it zoomed in on her purse with its telescopic sensor. The sensor switched to X-ray mode, looked inside the purse, and spotted the shard Sam had given her.

"*Target acquired,*" Wheels whispered in the Decepticon language, and followed her.

DIEGO GARCIA AIR BASE

In the middle of the Indian Ocean, a Blackhawk chopper came in for a landing on a small island. National Security Advisor Theodore Galloway stepped out. Galloway looked part politician, part cowboy. Major Lennox and Master Sergeant Epps stood there, waiting to greet him.

"Director Galloway," Lennox said. "Honor to have you onsite, but you're not on the access list—"

"I am now," Galloway interrupted. He snapped open a letter. "Presidential order, Major. My message is for your classified space buddies."

Galloway walked past him. Lennox eyed the man, his expression hostile. "Nice guy," Epps said sarcastically.

Lennox snorted.

Nearby, a C-17's rear door lowered and several Autobots rolled out, Optimus Prime in the lead. The Autobots, Galloway, and now Lennox all headed for a huge hangar. A couple of Smart Cars drove toward them, and the Twins immediately trans-scanned the tiny vehicles and changed, taking on the Smart Cars' appearances. They did a couple of happy donuts on the tarmac before following everyone else into the hangar.

Inside, as the doors slid closed, a big communications monitor lit up, showing the face of Admiral Morshower, chairman of the Joint Chiefs of Staff. He and Lennox, who knew each other, nodded greetings.

"Let's get started," Morshower said. "I believe you have some intel for us, Prime?"

Optimus Prime switched to his robot form, rising up to his full height. Galloway gasped.

"The last Decepticon incursion, unlike the six before it, left us with a message," Prime said. He replayed Demolisher's words: "The Fallen shall rise again. . . ."

"What does that mean?" Morshower asked.

"We don't know," Prime answered regretfully. "There might have been some answers in our recorded history, but that was lost when the AllSpark was destroyed."

"I'll tell you what it means," Galloway suddenly broke in. "It means that even though you said the Decepticons would leave our planet alone, they haven't. And with your AllSpark gone, there's only one conclusion. They're here for you. They're here to hunt Autobots."

Lennox said, "That's just jumping to conclusions. We don't know that!"

"I'll tell you what we know," Galloway snapped. "We know you sent an open invitation into space, and a number of Autobots have shown up because of it. Who else heard that message? Can you tell me? I didn't think so."

As Galloway spoke, hundreds of miles above their heads in orbit, a shadow crept across a U.S. military satellite. Soundwave, a Decepticon spy satellite. extended its metallic tendrils and connected to the military satellite, rapidly taking it over. Using the other satellite's telemetry equipment, Soundwave focused down toward

Earth, zooming in rapidly, until it locked onto the Diego Garcia Air Base.

As Galloway went on, Soundwave recorded everything.

"We know the enemy leader, classified 'NBE-1,' is rusting in peace at the bottom of the Laurentian Abyss, surrounded by military security and surveillance."

Soundwave immediately pinpointed the location to which Galloway referred.

"We know the only remaining piece from this AllSpark of yours is locked in an electromagnetic vault, here on one of the most secure naval bases in the world."

On Soundwave's internal monitors, schematics for the Diego Garcia base flashed up, scanning through to the vault. The shard of the AllSpark flashed in red.

"And we know that national security has been severely compromised." Galloway glared at Prime. "Let me ask you, Autobot leader, on behalf of the president: If we ultimately conclude that our security is best served by denying you further asylum on our planet . . . will you leave peacefully?"

Lennox gaped at him in disbelief.

Epps said, "You can't be serious!"

Optimus Prime remained calm as he responded. "Freedom is your right. If you make that request, we will honor it. But before your president decides, please ask him this: What if we leave . . . and you're wrong?"

As the word *wrong* echoed inside the hangar, a hatch opened in Soundwave's side and a shiny metallic sphere launched out. The pod rocketed toward Earth, glowing white-hot as it burned through the atmosphere, and splashed down into ocean waters.

Right off the coast of the Diego Garcia Air Base.

The Witwicky family pulled up in front of the college dorm, amid dozens of other vehicles off-loading eager freshmen. Sam got out, looking around a little goggle-eyed, and slowly walked toward the dorm. His parents followed.

"Look at this place!" Judy said, her voice bubbly. "I feel smarter just standing here!"

Ron grinned. "Smells like forty thousand a year to me. Go on up, Sam, we'll bring the bags. Go check out your room."

Sam needed no further prompting. According to his official paperwork, he was in room 312, so he bounded up the stairs and located the room in question, passing other students and a few parents along the way.

When he got there, Sam paused in the doorway, double-checking the room number. "Oh, boy," he muttered.

The room looked as if a tornado had hit it. Books, clothes, and random computer parts lay everywhere, and in the middle of it all, hunched at a computer desk, was a skinny guy with a head full of curly black hair and the thinnest moustache Sam had ever seen. The skinny guy turned to face him. "Hey. You must be Sam? I'm Leo. How's it goin', man?"

Sam stepped forward and shook Leo's hand. "Uh . . . what's up?"

"Hope you don't mind, I set up the crib. This is my corporate headquarters! Future Internet billionaire, that's me. The-totally-real-deal.com— you've heard of it, right?"

Sam's forehead wrinkled. "Uh . . . no . . ."

"News of the weird, man! Especially when it comes to *giant robot* weird! I got the market cornered . . . except for totally-real-giant-robots.com. . . . Guy stole my idea! Calls himself Robo-Warrior. Man, I *hate* that guy."

Leo talked so fast that Sam was having a hard

time keeping up. "So, uh, I guess I'll take the side of the room with the empty bed?"

"Sorry," Leo said. "Already claimed that side. Listen, I checked your file. You're poor, I'm poor, let's fix that! You work for me now!" Leo put his arm around Sam's shoulders and made a grand gesture with his other hand, as if pointing to a huge imaginary sign. "World's youngest Internet billionaires, you and me! Our names in lights! Whaddaya say?"

Leo's computer made a *bonk* sound. He rushed over to it and clicked a link that had just shown up in email. "*Aaargh!* Robo-Warrior did it again! He scooped me on footage . . . giant robots in Shanghai, from just last night! Man, I *really* hate that guy!" Leo straightened up and turned back to Sam. "You a tech-head?"

"Well, yeah."

"So we're compatible. Got a girlfriend?"

"Yeah." Sam didn't know what to make of this guy. He started wishing he'd been assigned another room.

"Okay, no poaching each other's girlfriends. Agreed?"

"Uh . . . okay, yeah . . ."

Just then both Sam and Leo noticed a super-cute blonde girl unlocking the door to the room directly across the hall from theirs. Leo whacked Sam's arm and said, "Oh, yeah. *Es la casa de las chicas en fuego. . . .*"

Starting to get a little numb from Leo's chatter, Sam said, "Uh . . . what?"

Leo jerked a thumb toward the blonde, who disappeared into her room. "I might have, ah, adjusted the housing database to put the hottest girls on our floor. And speaking of girlfriends? That's my next one right there. So hands off."

The blonde girl came back out, paused, and flashed a dazzling smile at Leo and Sam. "Hi."

Leo pounced on the opportunity. "*Wel*-come! Leo Ponce de Leon Spitz, the-totally-real-deal.com."

But the blonde girl looked right past Leo, turning up the wattage on her smile as she focused on Sam. "I'm Alice."

It took Sam a second to remember his own name. "Sam," he finally mumbled.

Leo interposed himself between Alice and Sam and repeated, "Leo."

Alice said, "Hi, Sam."

Getting impatient, Leo said, "He has a girlfriend."

Alice's eyebrows twitched up. "Lucky guy." Turning, with one last flash of that gleaming smile at Sam, Alice sauntered away down the hall.

Leo turned to Sam, scowling, and jabbed a finger at him. "It's on, Sammy-boy."

Sam spread his hands in a gesture of helplessness. "I have a girlfriend!"

Leo narrowed his eyes, grumbled, and sat down at his computer again, pointedly ignoring his new roommate.

Wondering exactly what had just happened, Sam went to find his parents so he could tell them good-bye and wish them well on their trip to Europe.

As the sun set over the Indian Ocean, the metallic pod that Soundwave had ejected began to change shape. Moving closer to the shore, the pod grew legs . . . then a head . . . and finally a tail, as it became a gleaming metallic version of a panther. Its name was Ravage, and it was on a mission.

Clinging to Ravage's underside was another Transformer—a tiny, spiderlike Decepticon called the Doctor. Ravage bounded over the base's cyclone fences and raced toward the supposedly impenetrable vault that held Optimus Prime's shard of the AllSpark. Ravage leaped up to the roof, and the Doctor zipped to an air shaft.

Seconds later the Doctor emerged. Clutched in its many-jointed limbs was the shard. Alarms went off as the theft registered on the base's security systems, but it was too late. The Doctor attached itself to Ravage again, and Ravage took off like a rocket, disappearing into the setting sun.

Uncertain, Sam followed Leo across the quad toward the sound of a party in full swing.

"First party's the game changer," Leo said. "We're hunting in the wild now. This is where freshman reputations are made."

"I can't really stay long." Sam checked his watch. "I've got a webcam date with my girlfriend."

"Well, while you play smoochie-poo with your laptop, I'm gonna be minglin' with the ladies."

Sam figured if he kept a close eye on the time, it couldn't really hurt to hang out for a little while. He followed Leo toward an enormous house with white columns and a huge second-floor balcony. College students seemed to be everywhere, laughing, dancing.

Might even be fun.

Half an hour later, while Leo was off trying to chat up a sorority girl, Sam stood near the punch bowl, feeling out of place. He couldn't pin down exactly why, but something wasn't right. His eyes drifted over to a plate of cupcakes near the punch. The music and voices and laughter all seemed to fade. Sam went to the cupcakes, dipped a finger in some frosting, and started drawing symbols on the tablecloth.

The same strange symbols he'd seen in his head when he touched the AllSpark fragment. *What do they mean . . . ?*

Sam's trance broke off when a voice next to his ear said, "Let me guess: art major."

He turned and found himself nose to nose with Alice, his across-the-hall neighbor. "Oh! This—no, I'm—just getting punch."

She laughed. "It's Sam, right?"

"Well, according to my parents, anyway." *Alice*—her name was Alice. Standing this close to him, Alice made it awfully hard to think straight.

Her eyes sparkled. "Would you like to dance, Sam?"

He sputtered, trying to put some words together. "Oh, hey, y'know, that'd be great—I mean, hypothetically—but, it's just, I—"

She laughed again. "Relax. I know you've got a girlfriend. I've got a boyfriend at home myself, back in Orlando. This would just be . . . pretend. Just for a dance. We could pretend to be boyfriend and girlfriend. That's not against the rules, is it?"

Sam sputtered again and glanced at his watch. Right now, he knew, Mikaela would be checking to see if he was online, and he was *so* not online. Suddenly a car alarm started blaring from outside.

A *familiar* car alarm.

A boy stomped in from the balcony and shouted, "Who drove the yellow Camaro? It's parked on the hedge!"

Close to panic all of a sudden, Sam chattered at Alice, "Sorry-I-have-to-go-I'll-see-you-around!"and bolted for the door.

Outside, Bumblebee was planted squarely in

the middle of the frat house's carefully landscaped hedgerow. Sam sprinted for the driver's door. "What is this? What're you doing here?"

He jumped behind the wheel just as Leo came out the front door. Leo's eyes bugged. "You have wheels? Bro, why you holdin' out on me?"

But Sam had already slammed the car into reverse, and he was about to peel out of there when the passenger door suddenly opened and Alice jumped in. "No way! This is your car?"

Completely jangled, Sam muttered, "No—yes—sort of. So I'm gonna drive it now . . . away." He backed up, jammed the gear shift forward, and pulled away, just as Leo caught a glimpse of Alice in the passenger seat.

The last sound Sam heard from the party was Leo's fading voice: "DUDE! That's SO not cool!"

Still unfamiliar with the town, Sam had no idea where he was going as he cruised away down the street, but Alice didn't seem to mind their lack of a destination.

"I love Camaros. My first car was my Dad's fuel-injected '92 Z-28!"

"Maybe this isn't the best time for . . . stories."

Sam was a lot closer to panicking than he wanted to be.

Then, adding to the impending panic, Alice's seat back suddenly flattened—and just as suddenly slammed forward, bashing her face straight into the dashboard.

"No!" Sam shouted. "That is *so* uncalled-for—"

But before Alice could even gather her wits, a cloud of green antifreeze sprayed out of the vents, directly into her face. "Alice, I'm so sorry! There was a . . . a recall on this model . . . that I paid no attention to. . . ."

The car came to a stop at the curb, and Alice opened her door, still sort of dazed. "It's okay," she said unsteadily. "I think I'll just . . . walk back to the dorm . . . from here." She got out and wobbled away down the sidewalk.

In the car, Sam pounded on the steering wheel. "That was *way* out of line! What're you even doing here?"

The radio kicked on and tuned to what sounded like a briefing. "The situation on the ground has changed. . . . A soldier's duty is to follow orders."

"Orders? What're you talking about?"

Another rapid re-tune on the radio produced a sound bite from an old war movie. "The commander has requested to see you, sir. There's no time to waste."

"Commander? *What* commander?"

The graveyard was located maybe a mile from the college campus. Bumblebee pulled through the gate and followed a narrow road around a hill and upward, to a section lined with very old, very large crypts. Sam got out, looking around sort of nervously, and jumped when a voice spoke from the shadows—a voice he recognized.

"Hello, Sam," said Optimus Prime. The Autobot leader had been crouching, hidden, but now he stood and walked over to Sam and Bumblebee before dropping to one knee.

Sam didn't know what to think. "You won't even give me a day in college? Not one day?"

His voice grave, Prime said, "A fragment of the AllSpark was stolen."

That shocked Sam into a semblance of calm. "What do you mean, stolen? *Decepticon*-stolen?"

Prime nodded. "We placed it under human

protection at your government's request—as a gesture of good faith. I am here for your help."

"*My* help? I thought you had things handled? I thought we had peace?"

The huge Transformer sighed. "We've kept much from you, Sam, because you deserve a normal life. But some of your leaders believe we've brought vengeance upon your planet. They must be reminded—*by a human*—of the trust we share."

Sam blinked a few times. "What are you asking me to do?"

"Speak for us. Stand with us."

Sam couldn't believe his ears. He let out a shaky little laugh. "Hold on—you want me to leave college? I just got here! I worked my whole life for this!"

"Fate rarely calls upon us at a moment of our choosing."

"But this isn't my war!"

"I fear it will be. And I don't want our planets to share the same fate." Prime looked off into the distance. "We lost whole generations. Until there was no one left to tell us of our origins ... or destinies. . . ."

Sam made a couple of false starts before he found the words he wanted. "Just . . . just listen to me for a second. I wanna help, I do. But I'm not some alien ambassador, okay? I can't even talk my way into a new roommate. I'm just a normal kid! It kinda all came clear to me when I was falling off a twenty-story building: I'm just not that guy! By the way? That hurt. You're not supposed to have back problems when you're eighteen, at least not in my species."

But Prime was undaunted. "Your only shortcoming is your lack of confidence."

Sam held up his hands. "Hold on—you're a forty-foot alien robot. If the government won't listen to you, they're sure not gonna listen to me."

"There is more to you than meets the—"

But Sam had heard enough. He barked out the words: "Stop! I *can't* help you!" Instantly he regretted sounding that harsh, and he softened his voice, but his resolve stayed firm. "Look, I'm sorry . . . you changed my life. But *this* is my life now. I belong here. Nothing I do is gonna make a difference."

Prime's head dipped. "I believe there is

greatness in you, Sam. Even if you don't."

Sam closed his eyes for a second. "You'll convince 'em, okay? You will. I mean, c'mon . . . you're Optimus Prime."

Sam turned and, with a last glance over his shoulder at Prime and Bumblebee, walked out of the graveyard.

NORTH ATLANTIC OCEAN

At the deepest point in the ocean—known as the Laurentian Abyss—Ravage skimmed over the waves, zeroing in on the location that Soundwave had sent to him. The Doctor still clung to his underside, with the shard of the AllSpark clamped in its spidery limbs.

When he reached the proper coordinates, Ravage plunged into the ocean and headed straight down. Down, down, down, a full ten miles below the water's surface, until he found the bottom—and the huge, dark shape, now covered with barnacles.

Megatron.

Ravage landed on his former leader's chest,

and the Doctor took the shard and skittered inside the blasted chest cavity. Seconds ticked by. Then the Doctor came rushing out as a searing light flashed from Megatron's steel insides.

And as the Doctor shouted, *"Hail, Megatron!"* in the Decepticon language, the giant Transformer's eyes blazed a seething bloodred, and his body began to move.

am and Leo sat in a huge auditorium, high up and in the back. It was the first class of Sam's first real day in college, and he felt pretty excited about it. Of course, with Alice sitting a few seats away—and stealing coy little glances at him every chance she got—he was also more distracted than he wanted to be.

The professor, a colorful character wearing a scarf and a fedora, began talking about space, gravity, and the universe, and Sam did his best to pay attention.

But when the professor asked the class to open their textbooks—which had the professor's own smiling face on the inside cover, since he had written it himself—Sam's mind suddenly went *way* beyond distraction.

The textbook was fascinating. Fascinating in a way no book had ever been before. Sam started flipping the pages . . . faster and faster . . . until he was literally fanning through them, absorbing the information just as quickly as the pages turned.

Leo leaned over and whispered, "Dude! What're you doing?"

Sam ignored him and shot his hand up. When the professor didn't call on him immediately, Sam waved his hand around frantically and almost bounced out of his seat.

"Ahem," the professor said, eyeing Sam. "Young man, no questions yet."

"Sorry, Mr. Colan," Sam practically shouted. "But I just read your book—"

"It's pronounced *Co-lahn*. And what do you mean, you just read my book?"

Sam left his chair and bounded down to the front of the auditorium. "Yeah, whole thing, just now. The thing is, though, Einstein was wrong."

While the professor gaped at him, Sam grabbed an erasable marker, went to the huge whiteboard, and started scribbling down alien symbols—the same ones he had seen in his head, the same ones he had drawn in cupcake frosting. All the while, Sam chattered: "Clear example for you: If you break down the elemental components of AllSpark and assume a constant decay rate, then extrapolate for each of the fourteen galactic convergences it took for the Sentinel Prime expedition to receive an echo on its signal, you end up with a formula for interdimensional energy creation that mass and light alone can't *possibly* explain. I mean, c'mon, guys, we learn this in drone stage—am I alone here?"

Sam looked over at the professor and discovered that the enraged man's eyes were bugging out of his skull. "You think you can mock me?" the professor shouted. "Professor Einstein and *me*?"

Suddenly Sam grew dizzy and disoriented. He felt as if he were waking up from a dream. "I'm—I'm sorry," he said, his voice fuzzy. "Did I say something?"

"Get out of my class!"

Sam's confusion shifted abruptly into fear, and he bolted out of the auditorium.

• • •

Deep in the stacks of the university's library, Sam scoured the titles, searching, not quite desperate. "A-ha!" He pulled a book down: *The Arctic Grail: A History of Expeditions.*

Sam took the book to a table and opened it, flipping the pages, this time at normal speed. It still didn't take him long to find what he was looking for. There, in black and white, was a record of his great-great-grandfather, Archibald Witwicky, the man who had discovered Megatron frozen in arctic ice. There was a photograph of his grandfather's lunatic drawings—of the symbols in Sam's head.

Sam sat down hard, his suspicions confirmed.

ICE PLANET

In Cybertronian jet form, Megatron blasted down out of the vastness of space and into the crimson atmosphere. The planet was barren, dead, devoid of life. The sides of the canyon into which the Decepticon flew were lined with strips of shredded steel, torn off during a catastrophic crashlanding.

At the end of the canyon, embedded in the rock, was a massive, ancient, foreboding starship: the *Nemesis*. The ship might have been as dead as the rest of the planet, but for a single blinking beacon.

Megatron entered the ship, switching forms as he landed. He faced a wall of Cybertronian sarcophagi—coffinlike containment vaults, each of which held a Decepticon, motionless and dormant. They were in cryo-sleep, waiting to be revived.

Starscream came to meet him. "Lord Megatron. At last! Soundwave informed me of your resurrection!"

Megatron stalked toward Starscream, who backed away fearfully. "You left me to die on the insect planet," Megatron snarled.

"Only to seek reinforcements, my lord. To find The Fallen's long-lost army—which fled Cybertron and crashed. In your absence, *someone* had to take command. . . ."

Megatron smashed his fist into Starscream's face, a mammoth, crushing blow that knocked the smaller Decepticon flat. "Even in death . . . there is no command but mine."

Megatron left Starscream where he had landed and moved onto the bridge of the *Nemesis*. A column of thousands of metal pins rose from the floor; their heights flowed and ebbed, and became the face of The Fallen.

"So," The Fallen said in a voice as dry and ancient as dust, "my apprentice has awakened and is reunited with my ship. While I assemble forces in other dimensions . . ."

Megatron took a humble tone. "I have failed you, Master."

"No. Our race may yet survive. There *is* another means of creating the AllSpark—one that was stolen from me long ago."

"But Master . . . the AllSpark was destroyed— by Optimus and his pet insect."

"Ah . . . but was it truly? Were *you* destroyed, Megatron?"

Megatron's red eyes lit up. "The AllSpark . . . lives still?"

"Its power and its knowledge can never be vanquished. It can only change *form* . . . be absorbed . . ." The Fallen hissed in distaste. "By the insect child who bested you. I have felt it."

Megatron growled. "The *boy*? Let me avenge myself, Master. Let me destroy him!"

"Patience, my apprentice. First he must be found. And when our war is won, as I have promised, I shall bestow upon you the powers of the Dynasty. You will have what you have always sought. For you, too . . . shall be a Prime." The Fallen paused. "Only one boy stands in your way."

The metal pins fell back into the floor as The Fallen's voice faded. Megatron turned to go—and came face to face with Starscream. "He spoke of the boy, Lord Megatron?" Starscream said humbly. "We are already watching. . . ."

Minutes later, fifteen sarcophagus units hissed as they opened. Megatron, Starscream, and fifteen Decepticons changed into flight mode and blasted off into the sky.

MIKE'S BIKES

It was three hours earlier for Mikaela in California than it was for Sam as she pulled up to her father's bike shop. She unlocked the door and dropped her purse on a counter—completely overlooking Wheels, the tiny Decepticon toy truck, lurking in the shadows.

She might have noticed him if her cell phone hadn't rung just then. She checked the screen before she answered: Sam. "You are so predictable," she said into the phone. "You stand me up on our first chat?"

On the opposite side of the country, Sam hurried across the campus, eyes darting around nervously. "'Mikaela, listen, something's happening to me!"

Mikaela smirked. "Oh, yeah? You got chest hair?"

"No, listen! This is serious! Remember my great-great-grandfather? How he got zapped by Megatron and started seeing those symbols?"

Mikaela's smirk vanished. "You *do* know we're on cell phones, right?"

"I'm seeing them, too!" Sam told her about what had happened in class. "It's been happening ever since . . ."

"What? Ever since what?"

"I touched that AllSpark splinter."

Behind Mikaela, Wheels switched forms, becoming a tiny robot. On the phone, Sam said, "You still have the splinter, right?"

"Yeah, it's in the shop safe."

Hearing that, Wheels spun toward the safe. He raised up on his tiptoes, pressing his head against the door. Mikaela dropped the phone, spun, and pinned him there with one hand, a blowtorch held in the other. Wheels squirmed and squealed, while Sam shouted from the phone, "What's going on? Mikaela!"

Holding the torch close to Wheels's face, Mikaela growled, "What're you doing here, you little freak?"

Wheels flailed about ineffectively. "Seek knowledge from AllSpark!" he howled. "Any piece! Every piece! Secrets of Dynasty must be reclaimed!"

Mikaela frowned. "What secrets? What knowledge?"

"The Fallen commands!" Wheels yelped. "Whatever form it has taken, we must find it! Show mercy, Warrior Goddess! I'm merely a salvage-scrap surveillance drone!"

"And I'm your worst nightmare." Mikaela slammed Wheels into a sturdy metal box and dropped a heavy crank case on top of it. The box shuddered and shook. She picked the phone back up.

"What was that?" Sam demanded. "What's going on?"

"Not on an open line," Mikaela said firmly. "Just be careful. I'm getting on a plane."

I n the hall outside Sam's dorm room, Alice turned the corner and saw Leo carrying a pizza box, about to open his door. "Alllliiiice," Leo said, grinning—but she smoothly put herself between him and the door.

"Sorry—Leo, is it? But I really need to talk to Sam alone."

Leo said, "But—but—but it's my room, too!" Before he could say anything else, though, Alice had slipped inside and shut the door after her. Glumly Leo headed down to the common room.

"I'll eat the whole pizza myself, then," he muttered.

Inside Sam's room, Alice found Sam sitting on his bed, his knees pulled up to his chest, staring blankly into space.

"Sam?" she said quietly.

He looked up at her, blinked, and said, "Oh, Alice! Whuh, what're you . . ."

She sat down on the edge of the bed. "I just want to talk."

In the TV lounge, Leo opened the pizza box, lifted a slice, and was about to take a bite when a commercial caught his eye. It was for a theme park in Orlando, Florida—and it featured Alice— pretty, blonde, across-the-hall Alice. Except it *wasn't* Alice—it was an animatronics robot that looked exactly like Alice.

Leo's eyes got big. "What is going on with *that?*" he whispered.

"Listen, Alice, now's not really a good time," Sam said, his voice shaky. She slid closer to him, her smile mesmerizing.

"I knew there was something special about you, Sam," Alice whispered. She leaned in. "You're, like, a *genius* or something."

And while Sam struggled to think of something

to say, three things happened quickly, one right after another. First, unseen by Sam, a metal tendril emerged from the back of Alice's head; at its tip was a dripping hypodermic needle. Second, the door opened, and Mikaela stood there with a suitcase and the metal box with Wheels in it. Third, the metal tendril whipped back inside Alice's head so fast that Mikaela didn't see it. All she saw was a beautiful blonde girl sitting on Sam's bed with him, leaning in for a kiss. The hurt on Mikaela's face quickly turned to anger.

"Great," she said. "Perfect. Thank you, Sam."

In a flash Sam sprang off the bed. "Mikaela! Okay, wait—this is not what it looks like. We were talking!"

Demurely, Alice asked, "Your girlfriend?"

"*Ex*," Mikaela snapped, spinning to head out the door.

"Mikaela, wait!"

But before Sam could reach her, Alice's tongue shot out of her head on the end of a five-foot-long metal tentacle, wrapped around Sam's neck, and slammed him into the wall beside the door. Mikaela turned, stunned and speechless, as Alice used the metal tentacle to hurl Sam across the room.

Without missing a beat, Mikaela scooped up the metal box and pitched it at Alice's head with all her might. The box clanged off Alice's skull and crashed out the window—and Alice's head swung *all the way around*, a full 360 degrees.

Leo appeared in the doorway at that moment, excited. "Sam, check it out! Your friend Alice? Something is seriously—" His words stopped in midsentence as Alice stood there, glaring at him with her head on backward. In a tiny voice, he finished, "—strange?"

Retracting like bizarre fish scales, Alice's "skin" peeled back to reveal a Decepticon head underneath. Sam lunged past her, shoving Mikaela and Leo out into the hall, and she fired a barrage of metal spikes that nailed into the door, just missing his head. "Go! *Go! Run!*" Sam shouted, and the three of them took off toward the exit.

"She's some kind of metal she-beast!" Leo jabbered, unhinged. "What've you gotten me into, Witwicky?"

"She's an alien robot! Now *move*!"

Leo went pale. "What? *What?* They're *real*?"

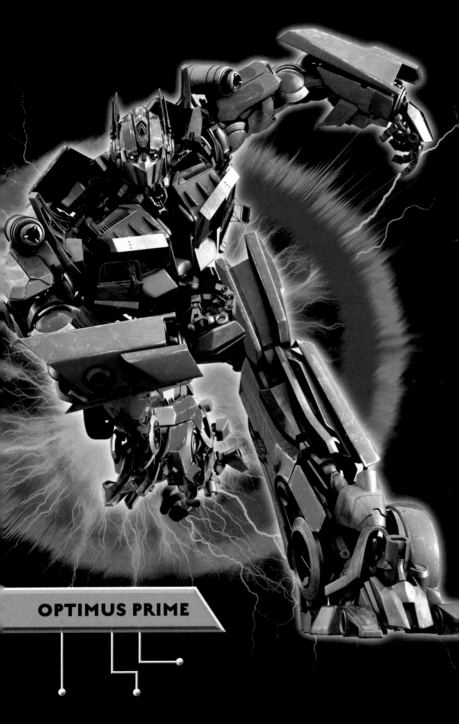

OPTIMUS PRIME

SKIDS

MUDFLAP

MEGATRON

STARSCREAM

RATCHET

BUMBLEBEE

THE FALLEN

"Stop talking and *run*!"

Behind them, Sam's door crashed out of its frame and slammed into the wall across the corridor. Alice walked out, looking human again, but with murder in her eyes.

Down the stairs, through the lobby, and across the quad, the three of them ran as fast as they could. A huge dark shape rose up in front of them: the library. "Hide in there!" Sam gasped.

Once inside, they tried to lose themselves amid the stacks, crouching down to hide in the early eighteenth-century poetry section.

Leo's whole body trembled. "I just saw her on TV! She's from the theme park! She's an Alice-in-Wonderland android!"

Sam looked around nervously. "They can copy anything mechanical."

Mikaela glared at Sam. "Yeah, it's called *trans-scanning*. So I see you were really missing me."

"What?" Sam frowned. "*I'm* the victim here! I couldn't get her away from me!"

It took Leo a second to catch up. To Mikaela he said, "Wait, how do *you* know about this scanning thing? Are *you* a real chick?"

She turned on him. "Exactly who are you?"

His chest puffed up out of sheer habit. "I'm Leo Ponce de Leon Spitz. I'm the *key* to this! They want me 'cause of the stuff about giant robots I post on my website!"

She sighed. "They don't want *you*. They want *him*."

Sam was beyond exasperated. "Could we hide quietly for a second?"

But it was too late. The stack beside them disintegrated as Alice exploded through it. She had shed her human skin completely and was now a six-foot-tall, full-metal Decepticon. Sam, Mikaela, and Leo all shrieked and ducked under a series of long tables, which Alice began tossing aside, one by one. Finally fed up with this, Alice changed one of her arms into a gun and fired a searing plasma bolt.

The bolt missed the three terrified humans, but it did blast a huge hole in the wall, and they wasted no time scrambling through it. In the parking lot, they quickly found a car that Mikaela could hot-wire. With no sign of Alice behind them yet, they drove out toward the street—and ahead of them, Mikaela spotted the metal box lying on the ground.

"Sam, grab that!"

He jumped out, snatched up the box, jumped back in, and slammed the door—just as Alice landed on the car's roof and pierced it with a long metal spine.

Mikaela rammed the car straight into a telephone pole.

Alice flipped off the top of the car and landed in a heap on the pavement. Before she could even get back up, Mikaela ran her over and sped off down the street.

Leo stared into the darkness behind them and then whipped around to confront Sam and Mikaela. "Why are you guys so calm?" he demanded. "Are you from the future? Did I send you back in time to save me?" He gave Mikaela a long look before turning to Sam. "And, dude, how could you cheat on a girl like this?"

Through gritted teeth, Mikaela said, "The girl's name is Mikaela." She eyeballed Sam for a second. "And that's an excellent question."

But before anyone could say anything else, a

massive helicopter swooped down out of the night sky—with the Decepticon symbol emblazoned on its belly—and pierced the car with a gigantic steel spike.

The chopper lifted the car completely off the ground and flew away into the night with it.

BROADWATER METAL WORKS

The foundry was dark, sprawling, and abandoned; once a place of industry, it was now more like a tomb.

The hot-wired car dropped through a gaping hole in the roof and fell a full thirty feet before crashing to the top landing of a broad staircase. All the airbags triggered as the car teetered, rolled, and finally came to a stop upside down.

An enormous steel scythe-blade sliced the car in half, lengthwise. The car fell apart, and Sam, Mikaela, and Leo tumbled out. They looked up at Starscream looming over them, scowling and silent. He took a step forward, trapping Mikaela and Leo in a corner.

Separated from them, Sam glanced around, trying to figure out what to do. He didn't get the chance, as Megatron rose up beside the staircase, his ruby eyes blazing.

"Remember me?" Megatron growled. "I remember you."

"Don't hurt my friends!" Sam begged. "*Please.*" Megatron paused, eyes narrowing, and Sam took the opportunity to bolt away, rushing down the stairs. Megatron reached one insanely long arm out and swatted Sam into the air. Sam tumbled down and came to rest on the concrete-slab floor, where Megatron pinned him in place with steel talons.

"You will pray for a sudden death, insect . . . while I . . . shall take my time. . . ."

With Sam pinned in place and Mikaela and Leo trapped, there was nothing any of them could do. As Sam watched, the Doctor came skittering across the floor, leaped onto his leg, and crawled up onto his chest.

"All we have to do is find out precisely what is in that brain of yours," Megatron said, pleased, as the Doctor unfolded an appendage that looked an awful lot like a hacksaw.

"No, no, no!" Sam shouted, squirming. "What d'you wanna know, I'll tell you! I'll talk! I'm talking!"

But the Doctor stopped, suddenly distracted by a small red dot glowing on its chest. Then a sniper shot hit the little Decepticon dead-on, blasting it to tiny bits. One of the foundry walls exploded as Optimus Prime crashed in. Megatron immediately flew one way, and Starscream the other, but Prime fired the cannons on his arms, and the shots slammed into both Decepticons.

"Run!" Prime shouted to Sam as Bumblebee appeared and hurried Mikaela and Leo away.

"Who's *this*?" Leo demanded.

"Bumblebee," Mikaela answered. "Your new best friend!"

Megatron sped outside, knocking another enormous hole in the foundry's wall, rocketing straight toward Optimus—who held Sam in his hand, attempting to get the boy to safety. Megatron slammed into Prime, knocking both Transformers down a steep embankment and into a forest. Prime managed to keep a safe grip on Sam, but only barely; when they came to a crashing stop at the bottom of the slope, Sam sprang away.

Prime and Megatron circled each other.

"Prime," Megatron hissed. "You risk it all . . . for a *child*?"

"For a *friend*."

Sam watched, transfixed, as Starscream blasted in as a jet, switched forms, and landed on Prime's right, just as Blackout, the helicopter Decepticon, touched down on Prime's left.

"There is another source of the AllSpark," Megatron shouted. "Hidden on this planet long ago. The boy can lead us to it. The Fallen decrees it!"

Prime's eyes narrowed. "Who is The Fallen?"

"You'll know when he arrives," Megatron snapped. "Is the future of our race not worth a single human life?"

Prime didn't hesitate. "You'll never stop at one."

The Decepticons sprang at Prime all at once— and in a truly dazzling display of combat, Prime held off all three of them. Gigantic blades flashed and machine-gun bursts of fire shredded trees around them, but Prime stood strong, a red-and-blue gladiator, blasting and bludgeoning like an engine of war.

"Run, Sam!" Prime bellowed. "Go now!"

Sam sprinted to the nearby tree line, but he couldn't abandon Prime.

One of Prime's arms burst apart and changed, turning into a huge blade, which he sank deep into the helicopter's housing. The chopper shorted out, sparks flying and dancing around it, and fell over sideways, out of the fight.

Megatron had taken that chance to circle around behind Prime.

And suddenly a twenty-foot steel spike burst through Prime's chest.

Sam screamed, "Nooo!"

Megatron retracted his blade, red eyes flashing like tiny suns, and sparks erupted from Prime's eyes and mouth as his system shorted. The Autobot leader tipped sideways like a felled oak and crashed to the ground.

"Run . . . boy. . . ." Prime whispered, before he lapsed into unconsciousness.

A colossal pulse blast came from out of nowhere and slammed Megatron square in the chest, knocking him off his feet. Sam whirled to see the Twins, Ironhide, Ratchet, and Sideswipe all racing toward them.

Ratchet shouted, "Bumblebee! Get everyone away from here!"

Bumblebee roared out of the trees and skidded to a stop in front of Sam; at the wheel, Mikaela beckoned to him desperately. Numb, Sam climbed inside, and Bumblebee roared away. Suddenly outgunned, Megatron and Starscream switched forms and blasted off, soaring into the sky.

High on a bluff on a deserted island, Starscream and Megatron came in for a landing.

"Organize our forces," Megatron said, fuming. "Reacquire the insect's location and intercept."

Starscream paused. "We've . . . lost the boy, Master."

Megatron turned on him. "I can't even rely on you to swat a simple insect."

Starscream put up his hands. "One insect among seven billion—he could be *anywhere*. There are no signals. The Autobots are hiding him."

Megatron considered that. "Then . . . we will

force the insects of the world to find him for us. . . . Start with the boy's parents."

Starscream immediately contacted Soundwave.

A fleet of naval ships patrolled the waters near the location of the former Operation Deep Six. Largest among them was an enormous aircraft carrier, the biggest kind of ship in the U.S. military—literally a floating city.

When the Decepticon sphere streaked out of the sky, no one saw it coming fast enough to react. The sphere slammed into the ship with a force so great that the entire ship split in half almost immediately. Sailors dove for lifeboats as the gigantic vessel began to sink.

Minutes later, as the stern end of the carrier came up out of the water, Megatron descended slowly from the sky. He perched on the ship's giant propellers, triumphant.

Before the aircraft carrier had even sunk into the ocean, every television screen in America—and then, seconds later, every television screen across the world—flickered with static and filled with Megatron's face.

"Insects of the human hive," he grated out in his gravelly voice, "now you know what your leaders have hidden from you. We are here. Among you. We can destroy your cities at will. If you wish them to remain standing . . . you will search for *this* boy."

The image on the screen changed to a shot of Sam.

In Paris, France, Ron and Judy sat in a small restaurant. A television played in a corner—and they both gasped in horror at the sight of their son.

Megatron's voice played over Sam's image so everyone could get a good, long look at him. "You've witnessed the destruction of your largest warship. There is no valor for those who try to resist. There is only annihilation. You have one solar day."

And the screen filled with roaring static.

Ron and Judy dashed out of the restaurant, rushing back toward their hotel. "We've gotta get a flight home and find him!" Ron panted. "Judy, tell him, call him. . . ."

But they didn't get the chance to do anything else. The surface of the street trembled, and a Decepticon, one of those from the *Nemesis*, erupted right in front of them.

The Decepticon grabbed them both, shoved them into a cavity built into its chest, and blasted off into the sky.

McGuire Air Base

Major Lennox and Master Sergeant Epps stood with the Autobots, watching solemnly as an Army helicopter descended. Optimus Prime was suspended underneath it, strapped to a platform hanging from steel cables. He hadn't regained consciousness yet.

As Prime was being placed in a hangar, a group of air force security officers came roaring toward the group in a cluster of Humvees, .50 caliber machine guns mounted on the back. The trucks circled the Autobots, guns aimed. Out of reflex, the Autobots pointed their own weapons right back.

"Whoa!" Lennox shouted, waving his arms

as he stepped between the officers and the Transformers. "Everybody stand down! We're on the same side!"

"That's not the case, as far as I'm concerned," said Galloway, as he stepped out of one of the trucks. He waved a piece of paper in the air. "And I've got a presidential order to back me up."

Galloway glared at both Lennox and Epps. "You and your little club are shut down. They've made this war *our* war, and now we're going to handle it in *our* way—by making battle plans and exploring diplomatic options."

Ironhide's voice was filled with disbelief. "You want to try to negotiate with Decepticons?"

"You won't need this anymore." Galloway ripped the rank patch off of Major Lennox's uniform. "But until you *do* actually leave, all of you—including that oversize paperweight you call Prime—are to get back to Diego Garcia. And *stay* there. Understood?"

Galloway didn't seem to care if they understood or not. He turned and walked back to the truck, and the security detail left with him.

"That guy is off my Christmas list," Epps said quietly.

Lennox tried not to grit his teeth when he responded. "Don't worry. . . . We'll get him back."

ABANDONED PRISON COMPLEX

Sam, Mikaela, Leo, Bumblebee, and the Twins all stared with glassy eyes and listened as terror alerts scrolled across Leo's smartphone. The director of the FBI stood there beside photographs of Sam, Mikaela, and Leo and told the nation that the three youths were wanted "for their own safety."

One of the Twins spoke, with a surprising lisp: "We can't reach any of the other Autobotth. All we know ith they're being forthed to go back to the bay . . . and they've got Prime with them."

"Get rid of that phone," Sam said hollowly. "They can use it to track us."

Leo groaned. "This represents last year's

profits." He dropped the phone and ground it under his heel.

Sam turned to Bumblebee. "Bee, I am so sorry. If only I had listened to Prime . . . maybe he wouldn't have gotten hurt."

Bumblebee looked at Sam with his big, moon-shaped eyes.

Sam turned to Mikaela. "I've got to turn myself in."

"What?" Her voice rose. "You can't do that! What, do you think if you give yourself up, Megatron will just leave the rest of the planet alone?"

Bumblebee played another recording—and it nailed Sam right in the gut. The voice of Optimus Prime said, "I believe there is greatness in you, Sam, even if you don't."

Sam took a deep breath. "Well, okay . . . okay, all right. If I'm *not* turning myself in, we've got to do something else." He faced the Twins. "Hey, do you guys know what these mean?" Sam went to a dust-caked wall and drew out the strange alien glyphs he'd been seeing in his head.

"That's the language of the Primes," the other

Twin said. "That's old-school. Way far back. 'Fore our time."

Leo spoke up. "Oh, boy. I think *I* know who can help." He sighed. "Robo-Warrior. My arch-nemesis. I saw some symbols like that on his website." Leo's shoulders slumped. "Time for a road trip."

NEW YORK CITY

am, Mikaela, and Leo all rode in Bumblebee, while the Twins in their Smart Car forms zipped around them on the highway. They crossed the Brooklyn Bridge, toward the skyscrapers looming ahead of them.

"How do you know this guy isn't just some twelve-year-old with a computer?" Sam asked.

Leo shrugged. "If he is, he's the smartest twelve-year-old in the world."

They stopped in front of a deli on Flatbush Avenue. "Wait outside," Leo said. "I'll go in and check the place out, then give you the go-ahead."

Leo walked in while Sam and Mikaela stood on the sidewalk, peering through the window. Sam froze in place as he saw the man Leo was talking to. He nudged Mikaela, gestured with his chin, and said, "I don't believe it."

Inside, working at the deli, was Agent Simmons, the Sector Seven operative who had given them such a hard time when they'd first met the Autobots.

At the counter, Simmons gave Leo a glance and said, "What'll it be, kid? Time is money."

"Robo-Warrior," Leo replied. "Know him?"

Simmons's eyes narrowed with recognition, and a growl started in his throat. "Leonardo Ponce de Leon Spitz. We meet at last."

Leo turned and beckoned to Sam and Mikaela, who walked inside. "It's him!" Leo said loudly. "Robo-Warrior! It's this guy!"

Simmons looked over and saw Sam and Mikaela, and all the color drained out of his face. "Meat store's closed!" he shouted. "Everybody out!" Grabbing Leo and Sam, he dragged them into a back hallway as Mikaela followed. "*You!* Again? Why're you doing this to me? You can't be seen here!"

Confused, Leo asked Sam, "Wait, you know this guy?"

Sam and Mikaela both nodded. "Yeah, we're old friends," Sam said.

Mikaela added, "We go way back."

"Old friends!" Simmons barked. "You cost me my job! There's no more Sector Seven, no retirement, no nothing! Now your face is all over the news, there's aliens all over the place—get lost! Vanish! G'bye!"

"But we need your help," Sam said earnestly.

That stopped Simmons. Slowly a grin spread across his face. "Oh, *really*. You need *my* help. How the wheel of justice turns! And why on Earth would I help *you*?"

"Three reasons," Sam answered. "One: You get to save the planet. That's big. Two: They'll give you your old job back. And three: 'Cause I'm sick of all this garbage! I've got giant robots shooting at me, an animatronics hot chick trying to—"

Mikaela punched him in the arm.

"Sorry . . . a mildly attractive robot tried to kiss me and then kill me, a crab-bot tried to dig out symbols in my brain with a hacksaw, and now I'm a wanted fugitive! You think *your* life sucks? Say the word—I'll run the meat store, and you can deal with the aliens!"

Simmons paused for a few seconds. Then he said, "Go back to the part about the crab-bot."

"Huh?"

"The crab-bot, you said it tried to get symbols outta your brain?" Sam nodded. Simmons jerked a thumb behind him. "You. Her. Him. Meat locker. *Now.*"

The meat locker in Simmons's shop turned out to conceal a trapdoor that led down into a basement. Sam, Mikaela, and Leo followed Simmons down a ladder into a room that was part bomb shelter and part retro 1970s museum. The place was filled with disco memorabilia.

Simmons jerked open a file cabinet, grabbed several folders, and dropped them onto a table. Photographs spilled out: images of ancient ruins, walls covered with hieroglyphs, clay tablets—all of them bearing the same alien symbols that Sam had been drawing.

"Any of these look like the symbols you saw?" he asked Sam.

"Where'd you get these?" Sam wondered.

"Grabbed them from S-7's vault before I left.

Fifty years of alien research, and it all means one thing: The Transformers have been here a long, long time. Like, caveman long. Same symbols showed up in ancient Greece, China, and Egypt. That means aliens were here way back then—and I think some of them stayed." He tapped a few photos of Industrial Revolution–era machines. "Remember steam engines? Cotton gins? The Model T? They've been hiding here all this time."

Looking at the photos, Sam felt his mind whirling. "Megatron said there was another source of the AllSpark on Earth. He thinks whatever's in my head will lead him to it."

"You asked the Autobots about this?"

"It predates them," Leo said sourly.

Simmons frowned. "Well, then we're out of luck. Too bad we can't ask a Decepticon."

"Actually," Mikaela said, "we *can*. Wait here, I'll be right back."

After retrieving the metal box from Bumblebee's trunk, Mikaela dropped it on the table with Simmons's photos and coaxed Wheels to come out. "Behave yourself," she told him pointedly. He cowered from her, nodding, eager to please.

Simmons couldn't believe it. "Spent my whole adult life looking for these things, and you carry one around like a Chihuahua."

Mikaela held up the photos of the ancient symbols. "Speak English! What do these mean?"

"Oooh," Wheels said, awed. "Language of Primes! Don't know, don't know! But—oh! *They* tell you!" The tiny robot pointed at the photos of antique machines, particularly one of an old bomber plane. "Seekers! Old Transformers! Old, old, old! Stranded, stuck! They search for something! Don't know what! From *old* times! *Thousands* of years!"

Simmons practically jumped up and down. "See? I told you they were here!"

Mikaela asked, "What are they? Decepticons? Autobots?"

"Both!" Wheels waved his hands in the air. "Battle-battle, race-race! They know symbols! They translate for you! I know where Seekers are!"

Wheels turned to a world map and projected laser pinpoints on ten locations. "The closest one's in Washington?" Simmons asked. "Do you have exact coordinates?"

Wheels looked around, and Simmons handed him a GPS device. Wheels jacked into it, downloaded information, and gave it back to Simmons.

Simmons chuckled. "Got news for you, gang. It's in a museum."

WASHINGTON, D.C.

It took some finesse, but Sam, Mikaela, Leo, and Simmons managed to hide themselves in the Smithsonian's aviation wing until after the Air and Space Museum had closed. Slowly and cautiously, making sure there weren't any guards nearby, they crept out of their hiding places. Mikaela took Wheels out of the backpack in which he'd been riding and set him on the floor.

"Follow! Follow!" Wheels squeaked, and he set off, heading deeper into the aviation displays. Mikaela handed Sam the film canister with the AllSpark shard inside it; Sam took it out and held it in the palm of his hand as they tracked after Wheels.

A minute later, the shard began to glow faintly.

Wheels pointed, squealing, "There! There!" The shard abruptly leaped out of Sam's hand, pulled as if by magnetism to a huge SR-71 Blackbird spy plane.

The shard clanked against the jet's fuselage, and a brief but intense pulse blast washed over the entire plane. Sam and Mikaela dashed under the jet, trying to retrieve the shard, but Sam stopped her when he saw the symbol on the bay door of the plane's landing gear.

It was the Decepticon king-head.

Sam said, "Oh, no."

At that moment the jet began to change—but they saw, as they sprinted out from under it, that the transformation was slow. The plane's metal parts ground against one another, and it made a wheezing sound, moving haltingly. Painfully.

Sam and Mikaela joined Leo and Simmons behind a Russian-made MiG fighter plane, where they hid and peeked out at the huge Decepticon.

The spy plane Transformer roared—a terrifying sound, like a thousand jet engines—but the roar quickly sputtered, coughed, and dwindled to barely a whistle.

"Aww, fragbottom," the jet muttered. "Low on juice ... why bother ... " He looked around, his red eyes narrowing, and in a louder voice demanded, "Who's there? *Show yourselves!* I'll annihilate each and every one of you! *Fleshlings?* Approach! Speak, or suffer my wrath!"

No one knew what to do. Sam took a few tentative steps forward. Uncertain, Mikaela followed, and when the huge Decepticon didn't immediately attack, so did Leo and Simmons.

The Transformer wheezed again, and his limbs trembled. A pair of lenses snapped out and down over his eyes as he peered down at the humans. "Name's Jetfire, you wretched bipeds," he said, his voice also trembling a little. "I'm on a mission—no time for chitchat. Behold me! Behold me and ..."

Jetfire seemed to forget what he was doing. Without further words, he turned and started walking toward a huge set of doors that led outside.

"Uh . . ." Simmons started. "You gettin' the festering feeling that something's a little off here?"

Mikaela watched as Jetfire retreated. "I don't

think he's going to hurt us."

Sam rushed after the Transformer, waving his hands. "Hey!"

Jetfire pushed open the doors and walked outside into an airplane graveyard; thousands of old military planes rested, row after row, in a vast concrete lot. Everyone, Wheels included, ran after him. "Wait!" Sam shouted. "Mr. Jetfire! Stop! We just wanna talk to you, please!"

Trudging along, muttering to himself, Jetfire suddenly stopped and spun around to face Sam. "Where am I going? Dag-blast it! What planet am I on, lad?"

"Um . . . Earth, sir."

Mikaela's eyebrows rose. "You . . . you don't remember where you are?"

Jetfire sighed. "Reach a certain mileage, milady, the old circuitry begins to fail you. *Arrgh* . . . is that pointless war still going on? Decepticons— such heathens and cowards. That's why I defected to the Autobots. Can't we all just get along?"

Jetfire looked down at his feet. Wheels, in truck mode, was driving figure-eights around the huge Transformer's feet like an excited puppy.

Jetfire picked Wheels up in one massive hand and squinted at him. "Look at you whippersnappers today, with your nano-servo gizmos. In my day, we were real robots!" Wheels chirped at him sharply, and Jetfire responded with, "Yes, yes, so I said. I changed sides."

Wheels switched forms. "Change sides? You can do that?" The tiny robot did a backflip off Jetfire's hand and landed next to Mikaela. She patted his head affectionately as he hugged her leg. "Wheels takes her side!"

Jetfire tried to stand up straighter but lost his balance, groaned, and sat down hard on the pavement. "Oh, bloody slagbucket," he said, disheartened. "Been scouring this rock for two thousand *years*! Got a mission, but I keep forgetting what it *was*...."

Sam moved closer to him. "Listen. If you can help me, maybe I can help you."

Minutes later—after Bumblebee and the Twins had joined them—Sam had scratched column upon column of alien symbols in the dirt at the edge of the lot. "It just keeps coming," he said distractedly.

"I could write it forever. Whatever it is, Megatron wants it—him and some Transformer he called The Fallen."

Jetfire had hauled himself over, squinting down at the symbols through his lenses as Sam wrote—but now his eyes suddenly got huge. "The Fallen? As in *The* Fallen? My boy, you may have saved us all! It's all there in your transcriptions! *Now* I remember what I was seeking! The Dagger's Tip! The Kings! And the key!"

Sam stood up. "What key? What dagger?"

"No time to explain!" Jetfire struggled to his feet. "We have to get there before I forget where we're going!"

"Going?" Simmons barked. "Going where?"

But Jetfire had no further words for them. He tensed up, his whole body straining, and suddenly his chest-plate opened, revealing the spark within. Jetfire's spark flashed a brilliant blue, and erratic forks of lightning began cascading off of him, forming a web—a web that joined and curved inward, creating an artificial black hole. "Everyone gather close and don't move!" Jetfire bellowed.

"What's going on?" Sam shouted, holding Mikaela tightly.

"Post-Dynastic technology," Jetfire shouted back. "Discontinued in later models! Prone to catastrophic failure!"

"Catastrophic?" Leo shrieked, his voice raising several octaves. "What do you mean, 'catastr—'"

And then everyone disappeared in a blinding blue-white flash.

EGYPT

Two at a time, the group fell out of the
sky, thumping onto desert sand. Jetfire
himself was the last to appear, coming to
rest flat on his back on a large perched rock.

After making sure everyone was okay, the
group approached Jetfire, with Sam in the lead.
"Okay, so . . . where are we?" he asked.

Jetfire didn't seem to hear him at first.
"Whew . . . haven't opened a transdimensional land
bridge in *ages*. Hmmm, thought there'd be some
water near here. I must be off by a little bit. Oh,
my aching hull."

"That's great," Simmons said, "but you left out
the part about where we are!"

"Egypt," Jetfire told them, a note of impatience

in his voice. "I already explained all that."

"You explained it in your mind!" Simmons exploded. "Your own demented, twisted mind! I demand a debriefing, right now!"

Jetfire raised one hand and gave Simmons a flick, sending him tumbling down a sand dune. "Why do you think The Fallen sent me here in the first place? Your symbols, boy. They're a *story*, the genesis of our race. Of how we were divided . . . by The Fallen himself."

Everyone listened closely to Jetfire as Simmons made his way back up the dune.

"I should tell you this quickly. The land bridge probably drew the kind of attention we don't want."

"We're listening," Sam said.

"All right. Long ago I was a Seeker, me and several others. And I shall tell you what we sought . . ."

A lens opened in Jetfire's chest, and he projected a holographic image into the air: the AllSpark, floating in a cavern, surrounded by twelve enormous Transformer protoforms.

"See, in the beginning, we were ruled by

the Dynasty of Primes—the first Transformers, created by the AllSpark to bring life to Cybertron."

A silvery plasma dripped from the AllSpark, quickly taking shape as a daggerlike spike with a crystal in its center.

"The AllSpark forged the Matrix of Leadership. Its power would be used to activate a great machine. . . ."

The image changed, becoming a representation of a huge machine that The Fallen had built on Earth thousands of years ago, though it was known to none of the humans.

Jetfire continued, "A machine built to destroy suns and collect their raw power."

"Wait," Sam interrupted. "Destroy suns? Like, blow 'em up?"

Nervously, Mikaela said, "We kinda need our sun."

"And your world should have been spared," Jetfire sighed. "But The Fallen *hated* organic life and would have wiped out your species. He defied the other Primes and deactivated them, one after another. Only a single Prime escaped, and he took the Matrix of Leadership with him, finally sealing it—and himself—in a tomb, here on Earth."

All four humans exchanged glances. It was too much information to process quickly.

Jetfire went on. "The great machine was left abandoned." The holographic image changed, showing a civilization spreading out around the enormous construct, which quickly became buried under sand. Recognizable structures grew: temples, palaces. *Pyramids*.

"Your race grew—and buried our history. But somewhere beneath this desert lies the Matrix . . . and the machine. The Fallen intends to return—to activate it." The holographic image faded out.

Mikaela balled up her fists. "Then how do we stop him?"

"Only a Prime can defeat The Fallen," Jetfire replied. "That is why he returned to Cybertron to wage war. He deactivated all direct descendants of the Prime Dynasty, except for one who was hidden away. An orphan—forever unaware of his destiny."

It clicked in Sam's head. "Optimus *Prime*." Then an even crazier thought occurred to him. "Jetfire! You said the Matrix was made by the

AllSpark. Right? Well, Optimus Prime is here, but he's badly hurt! If the Matrix could reactivate this sun-destroyer machine . . . could it reactivate Optimus Prime?"

Jetfire scratched his head, thinking. "Well, yes, I suppose it could. In theory." He looked around, as if suddenly unsure of where he was again. "Listen, I can tell you what your symbols mean, but I'm afraid you'll have to go it alone from here. My old wings would attract too much Decepticon attention. . . . Plus, I need a nap."

"What do they mean?" Simmons asked eagerly.

Jetfire cleared his throat. "'When dawn alights the Dagger's Tip . . . Three Kings will reveal the doorway.' Now, if you'll excuse me." The huge Transformer rolled over on his side, curled up, and started snoring.

Sam turned to the rest of the group. "We've got all the clues we're going to get from him. Let's get moving while we figure this out."

An hour later, as Bumblebee and the Twins made their way along a desert highway, Simmons closed his cell phone. "Okay, here's what my CIA contact says: Ancient Sumerians used to call the Gulf of Aqaba 'the Dagger.' It's part of the Red Sea—divides Egypt and Jordan like the tip of a blade. Twenty-nine-and-a-half degrees north, almost thirty-five east." He punched the coordinates into his GPS device and got a satellite photo of the location. "There are old ruins there now. Looks totally abandoned."

Ahead of them, the Twins came to a border-crossing checkpoint. Both cars got waved through immediately.

"Can we do this? This checkpoint?" Leo asked, his voice rising. "I don't think I have my ID!"

"Relax," Simmons said. "Just act like you know what you're doing."

Sam tried that, giving the border guard a polite smile—and, about a half second too late, noticed the security camera aimed straight at him.

He whipped his face away, but not before it had been clearly captured and transmitted. With a sudden knot in his stomach, Sam said, "Well, now the whole world's going to know where we are." It took all of his effort not to pound on the steering wheel as he pulled away from the checkpoint.

The four of them rode in silence for nearly a minute. They knew that Sam's face had suddenly popped up on monitors at Interpol and at the CIA. And if Earth's authorities knew where they were, the Decepticons would, too.

"We've gotta get off the road," Simmons said. "We're compromised, we've gotta hide till nightfall."

"We *can't*," Sam replied. "We're running out of time! We've got to send a message to Lennox—get him to bring Optimus to the Dagger's Tip."

Speaking more calmly than the rest of the group had come to expect from him, Leo said, "No, we can't. You're on the worldwide wanted list. Try calling him on the base, and they'll track you in seconds."

Sam thought about that. "Who says we gotta call him on the base?"

LENNOX HOUSEHOLD

 arah Lennox and Monique Epps watched as Sarah's two-year-old played in the backyard with Monique's son and four daughters. Sarah had made lemonade, and she was just reaching for her glass to take another sip when her cell phone rang from inside the house.

"'Scuse me," Sarah said as she got up out of the wicker lounge chair.

Monique waved one hand. "Go right ahead. I'll just stay here and mind the flock."

Inside the house, Sarah found the ringing phone and answered it. "Hello?"

The voice on the other end of the line was male, young, and slightly out of breath. "Hi, my name is Sam Witwicky, and I *really* need your help. . . ."

• • •

Forty-five minutes later, at McGuire Air Base, Lennox and Epps walked quickly toward a C-17 cargo plane. Lennox asked, "Sarah and Monique got you these coordinates how, exactly?"

Epps grinned and shook his head. "They knew everybody'd be listening—and they were right, Galloway was standing right there—so Monique pretended like she was talking about getting plastic surgery. Rattled off all these numbers, supposed to be weights and measurements and costs and such."

"And nobody picked up on that?"

Epps shook his head again, his grin even wider. "My baby should win an award, pullin' that off."

"I'll say." The two men arrived at the C-17, just as the crew finished loading Optimus Prime's inert body into its cargo hold. Lennox scribbled a note and handed it to the base's air boss.

"Sergeant, once we're airborne, Admiral Morshower has to get this information ASAP. I take full responsibility."

The sergeant frowned at the paper; then he frowned at Lennox. "But you're just transporting the Autobots back to Diego Garcia."

Lennox clapped the man on the shoulder. "That's our registered flight plan, yes. You'll make sure that note gets where it needs to go, right?"

The air boss nodded, then turned and walked away. Lennox and Epps went to find the C-17's pilot. "We ready to do this?" Epps asked. "You'll have to give them a reason as to why we're changing course."

The pilot grinned. "I'll think of something. Now strap in—we've got a long way to go."

WASHINGTON, D.C.

At the Pentagon, Admiral Morshower sat at his desk, fuming. He knew Galloway had crippled their defense efforts by disbanding his combined military and Autobot team, but he couldn't think of anything to do about it.

Just then, an aide knocked on his door. "Mr. Chairman?"

Morshower waved him inside. The aide silently handed him a faxed note. Morshower unfolded the piece of paper and read it. As the meaning of what he was reading sank in, he began to get excited. *Really* excited.

The fax read: FROM LENNOX—29.5° N / 34.88° E—GET READY TO BRING THE RAIN.

Morshower fixed the aide with a calculating stare, his mind whirling. "Lennox knows something. We have to be ready to back him up if this goes hot. . . . Have NSA task our keyhole satellites to target these coordinates on a thirty-minute rotation."

"Yes, sir."

Morshower stood. "Put CENTCOM on alert—I want their B-1s and F-22s on Alert 5, loaded and ready."

"Yes, sir!"

"And raise PACFLEET, too—move the Roosevelt Battle Group at flank speed into the Red Sea. I want it on station ASAP."

"Yes, sir!" The aide turned and practically ran from the office.

Far, far overhead, Soundwave received a message from Megatron. "Inform The Fallen," the Decepticon leader's voice rasped. "The boy has been found. The time has come for my master's arrival."

EGYPT

The night before, Simmons had sneaked the group into an abandoned tourist center. It had no water and no power, and it barely counted as shelter at all, but Leo and Simmons both slept like logs inside.

Outside, with Bumblebee and the Twins not far away, Sam and Mikaela sat side by side, staring at the majestic pyramids. Stars filled the predawn sky overhead.

"Just a few days without me," Mikaela said. "See how things fall apart when we're not together?"

Sam took a breath to answer and then looked away. "I don't know. Being my girlfriend has turned out to be pretty hazardous to your health."

She leaned closer to him. "Yeah, well. Girls like

dangerous boys."

He turned to face her. Looked into her deep, entrancing blue eyes. "You know I'm gonna break you," Mikaela breathed. "So you might as well just say it."

Sam gave her the tiniest grin. "Say what? Say *it*? No, I know what you're asking me to say. But right now? Not really gonna feel natural. I mean, I *can* say it, it's not that I *can't* say it...."

Mikaela sat back, exasperated. "Sam Witwicky, I cannot *believe* you. We're sitting in front of these three pyramids, at one of the most romantic spots on *Earth*, under a full moon and stars, and you can't even admit you love me!"

Sam blinked, his eyebrows drawing together—and a thought flashed in his head like a lightning bolt. "Pyramids and stars . . ." He turned and peered up into the night sky at the star formation known as Orion's Belt—with *three stars in a row*.

Sam jumped up. "Pyramids and stars!"

Mikaela got to her feet as well. "Sam, what are you thinking? Or is this just your way of ducking out of the conversation?"

By way of answering, Sam grabbed her wrist and said, "Come with me." He pulled her back toward the tourist center. "Wake up! Simmons, Leo, wake up! I know where the Three Kings are! Our astronomy class . . . the textbook . . . page forty-seven. Remember?"

Leo sat up, rubbing gunk and sand out of his eyes. "No, I do *not* remember! I was only in college for two days!"

Sam rushed up to the center's rooftop. When the rest of the group had joined him, he pointed into the sky. "Orion's Belt! Those three stars— they're also called the Three Kings! Now, look, the Pyramids of Giza—right under the three stars— built by three Egyptian kings! It's like an arrow staring us right in the face!"

Simmons slowly realized Sam was making sense. "They all point due east, where the sun rises. 'When dawn alights . . .'"

Mikaela caught on as well. "'Three Kings will reveal the doorway.'"

Sam pointed at a mountain ridge about fifty miles away. "There. That ridge. The tomb's gotta be over *there*."

An hour and a half later, Sam, Mikaela, Leo, Simmons, Bumblebee, and the Twins arrived at a

113

tomb built into the side of a rocky mountain. The doorway to the place was a darkened archway at least sixty feet high. Bumblebee looked tiny in comparison.

"Weird," Mikaela murmured, looking around once they had gone inside. They stood in a huge chamber, but instead of Egyptian hieroglyphics, the walls were covered with Roman murals. Caesar and his conquering armies.

There was no sign of anything related to Transformers—past or present.

"Great!" Leo shouted. He bent and picked up a fist-sized chunk of broken pottery. "Just great! All this way for nothing!" He gave Simmons a dirty look. "Thanks, Robo-Warrior! Good job!"

"Grow up, kid," Simmons snapped back. "Life isn't a cushy college campus where they fix you three meals a day. Real life is *heartbreak*. Real life is *despair*."

Leo's face paled. "How did you ever work for the government?" he shouted. "Seriously, who would ever hire you? I want to see some kind of documentation that proves you were once entrusted with an actual job!"

And he threw the chunk of pottery straight at Simmons's head.

Simmons ducked out of the way—and the pottery cracked against the wall of the tomb, breaking off a piece of the Roman mural the size of a dinner plate.

Everyone stopped dead, staring at the wall, and Sam's eyes lit up.

Underneath the mural, etched into a wall made of metal, was one of the alien symbols Sam had come to know so well.

It took Bumblebee only a few minutes to break loose a much larger section from the wall, revealing more alien symbols laser-etched into a seven-foot section of metalized ribbing.

"Romans painted over the alien symbols when they conquered Egypt, just as they painted over the hieroglyphics," Simmons said quietly.

"This is it," Sam breathed. "This is *it*!"

Bumblebee motioned everyone back, changed his right arm into a plasma cannon, and fired into the metal wall, blowing a respectable-sized hole in it.

Sam held his breath as he stepped through

the hole and into a huge metal tomb. There, in the middle, as if waiting to be picked up, was the Matrix of Leadership. Mikaela touched Sam's shoulder. Seconds after it had been exposed to air, the Matrix crumbled into fine black sand.

"No," Sam said. "No. This is *not* how this ends."

A faint sound reached them from outside. Simmons ran to the huge doorway. "C-17s!" he shouted. "They're air force! They're ours!"

Leo entered the tomb and gaped at what was left of the Matrix. "Sand—are you kidding me? We did all this for worthless *sand*? Are we done now? Can we go?"

"No!" Sam said, more to himself than anyone else. He whipped off his shoe, pulled off his sock, and started scooping the black sand into it. "They hid it! We didn't come here for nothing! We're here for a reason, you understand? Everyone's after me 'cause of what I know, and what I *know* is this is gonna work."

Mikaela winced. "*How* do you know?"

Sam stood, holding the sock. "Because I believe it."

PYRAMIDS OF GIZA

With perfect precision, Lennox and Epps's team parachuted out of the passing C-17s and into a deserted town of ruins on the edge of the Red Sea. They landed in a huge courtyard: the team of soldiers, Ironhide, Sideswipe . . . and Optimus Prime's inert form, still strapped to a transportation platform.

A British soldier ran to the top of the closest building and scanned the horizon. "Got visual!" he shouted. "Yellow team! Two kilometers out!" He pulled a flare gun from his belt and shot a signal flare into the sky.

Sam saw the flare from behind Bumblebee's wheel. "Over there! There they are!" Sam yelled.

Bumblebee increased speed.

Suddenly the road in front of them erupted with twin plasma bursts as Megatron and Starscream roared overhead in jet form.

As Leo screamed at the top of his lungs, the Twins zoomed ahead of Bumblebee, crisscrossing over the dirt road, kicking up a huge cloud of dust. With visibility cut to zero, the Decepticon jets couldn't find their targets, and their follow-up pulse blasts missed.

"Sam!" Lennox's voice came out of Bumblebee's radio. "Sam, can you hear me?"

Sam leaned toward the console. "Lennox! Yes! Do you—"

But suddenly there was a loud squelch and a *pop*, and nothing else came out of the speakers. Simmons growled. "That was an electromagnetic pulse."

"What does that mean?" Leo wailed.

As Sam sat back, disgusted, Mikaela said, "It means the bad guys just killed the phones."

Sam's eyes locked on the sky. "That might be the least of our problems."

Mikaela followed his line of sight. They both

watched as Decepticon orbs came hurtling down toward the deserted town ahead of them.

In a control center in Washington, Admiral Morshower stared at a surveillance monitor. "Do we have live feed from those coordinates?" he barked.

"Coming in now!" a technician told him. An image sprang into clarity on the monitor: a group of soldiers and six Autobots.

No Decepticons in sight. Morshower frowned. The technician said, "All quiet on the western front."

"Keep watching," the chairman ordered.

He had no idea that the digital feed had been received, doctored, and re-sent by Soundwave. At that moment, thirteen Decepticon warriors were actually advancing on Lennox, Epps, and the Autobots.

Bumblebee and the Twins arrived at the ruined town—but on the opposite side from the shore, still half a mile away from Optimus Prime. Megatron and Starscream roared overhead. Everyone piled out, and Sam clapped his hand on Bumblebee's hood.

"We gotta split up—Bee, you lead 'em away, and I'll get to Optimus."

Bumblebee's radio dialed up an army movie: "Sir, yes, sir!"

Simmons jerked his thumb at the Twins. "I'll help draw their fire. You get to those soldiers. Hope that dust works, kid."

Sam gave Simmons a genuine smile and shook his hand. "Thanks."

Simmons jumped into one of the Twins. "It's up to me," he said, talking to himself. "One man alone. Betrayed by the country he loves. Now he's its last hope in the final hour of need."

Suddenly the passenger door opened and Leo jumped in. "I'm coming with you!"

Simmons eyeballed him for a second. He put the car in gear, and repeated, "One man alone. . . ."

Sam and Mikaela raced into town along a row of excavation equipment that seemed to be just as abandoned as the rest of the place. They ducked behind a pillar as Megatron and Starscream roared by overhead—and when they saw the two gigantic planes bank sharply, they took cover inside a hut.

The growing roar of jet engines suddenly cut off, and the ground shook as a Decepticon landed right outside.

"As soon as they're gone, we run as fast as we can for Optimus," whispered Sam. But before they even got the chance to make a dash, the entire roof of the hut was torn away, revealing Starscream looming over them.

The huge Decepticon howled and pointed, and Sam and Mikaela both ran faster than they ever had before, sprinting away from the hut and down an alley. They knew their only hope was to lose Starscream in the maze of the town's ruined buildings. As they hurtled through a doorway into a tiny house, a huge pulse blast demolished the room right behind them. Sam and Mikaela both screamed and rushed up a stairway, which put them out on a roof.

"What do we do?" Mikaela gasped.

"Keep running!"

The two of them dashed across the rooftop and leaped across the gap to the next one, just as the building behind them exploded into shreds. Starscream burst up through the rubble, right behind them. They crashed through a window into an empty apartment, where they slammed into the floor, dazed.

In his control room, Admiral Morshower peered over a technician's shoulder at the satellite feed, which still showed only Lennox's group at the water's edge.

"Something's wrong. Get a spy drone to that site."

"Yes, sir!"

DESERT QUARRY

Simmons and Leo skidded to a stop in the bottom of a rock quarry, surrounded by construction equipment. Leo turned around and peered behind them. "They're not following us anymore. I don't think it's working."

But Simmons wasn't listening. He stared up at the top of the closest pyramid—where a blade of light suddenly seemed to cut the air itself, followed by a thunder crack and a shockwave that shook the desert floor. A wormhole opened in the sky. The Fallen himself appeared at the top of the pyramid.

Megatron flew in to land beside him. "Master. Your machine remains in place."

The Fallen roared, "Where is the Matrix?"

Simmons, who had dropped into an awestruck trance, snapped out of it when Leo grabbed his arm and pointed. The construction vehicles had all started up—*by themselves*—and bunched together, changing shape. But not just transforming—they were *combining*, becoming a Transformer much, much larger than any that the humans had seen before. Soon the machines had become a Goliath-sized wrecking crew.

The Twins' voice spoke through the radio, sounding terrified: "That's Devastator."

am and Mikaela recovered from their fall and made it out of the building, but the Decepticon pursuit was relentless. They dodged between buildings and darted down alleyways, but the explosions behind them never stopped. Sam risked a glance over his shoulder and saw something that made his heart lurch in his chest. Megatron had turned into a *tank*.

And he was firing at them now.

"There!" Mikaela pointed. Ahead of them, finally, Sam spotted Lennox.

"Go!" he panted, and they tried to run even faster.

DESERT QUARRY

I n the quarry, Devastator turned, lumbered toward the pyramid where The Fallen was perched, and began climbing. When he reached the top, The Fallen moved to one side, and Devastator lived up to his name: He started smashing the pyramid apart, sucking up the pieces into a glowing green furnace built into his chest.

And as he destroyed the Egyptian national treasure, something was revealed within the pyramid.

Watching from below, Simmons gasped. "It's the machine! What the plane was talking about— the sun destroyer! That pyramid was built right over it! We're sittin' right at the endgame!"

Frantically, Simmons pulled out his cell phone and started mashing buttons.

"I thought all the phones were dead," Leo said.

"EMPs only last so long," Simmons grunted. "There's something else going on here—some reason our satellites aren't picking up on all this. But my phone is also a radio, and if I monkey with the frequency . . ."

Suddenly a burst of static emerged from the phone. Simmons laughed, almost hysterically, and turned his bulging eyes to Leo. "Stay here! I'm gonna try something!" And before Leo could even respond, Simmons ran to the base of the pyramid and began climbing up, heading straight toward Devastator.

On the bridge of the USS *Roosevelt*, part of the American fleet awaiting orders off the coast of Egypt, a communications officer turned to the captain. "Sir, we have radio traffic coming in. I'm . . . not sure what to make of it."

"Put it through," the captain said. The static-filled signal emanated from nearby speakers.

"This is Captain Wilder, USS *Roosevelt*. Identify yourself."

Simmons struggled mightily, trying to climb the five-foot-high blocks of the pyramid with one hand, his phone gripped in the other. "Where in blue blazes are all our men?" he shouted. "We got three hundred satellites up there—are they all watching the weather?"

On the other end of the phone, Captain Wilder snapped, "Identify yourself! Who is this, and what are you talking about?"

Simmons gritted his teeth. "You're telling me no one knows what's going on here ... but me? Okay, then listen up! This is Agent Seymour Simmons, Sector Seven! Never heard of it? There's a reason! Now you wanna have a throwdown about my lack of clearance, or you wanna help me save a gazillion lives?"

Captain Wilder thought hard about that—for maybe a quarter of a second. "All right, Agent Simmons, I'm listening."

Simmons threw a wild-eyed glance above him at Devastator, who hadn't even noticed he was there. "Five clicks west of the Gulf of Aqaba we got ourselves an alien remodeling a pyramid! Our one hope is a weapon you've got on board: a rail gun. Shoots a steel projectile at Mach 7, am I right?"

Wilder's voice on the phone was audibly shaken. "That's . . . classified; how do you kn—"

"Never mind how I know! I'll radio exact coordinates in T-minus-five! Be ready!"

High overhead, Admiral Morshower's spy plane finally got within range and snapped a series of images. In his control room, Morshower's face turned beet red. "It's a trick! There are hostiles everywhere! Mobilize everybody!"

Hiding behind a row of pillars, Sam and Mikaela both saw it at the same time—what looked like a green-and-black swarm of locusts came rushing toward the shore from the gulf.

The fleet of ships had launched wave after wave of hovercraft and gunship helicopters. The hovercraft had reached land and off-loaded dozens of Abrams tanks, which moved into the town and immediately engaged the Decepticons. The air seemed to be made of noise and fire as the military unloaded on the evil aliens.

Under the cover of tank and helicopter fire, Lennox and Epps both made a dash for Sam and Mikaela, skidding into the dirt right beside them.

"We've got to get you both to cover!" Lennox shouted. "Follow me, and stick close!"

Sam saw where Lennox was pointing: a secure position about four hundred yards away. Off to one side—exposed and vulnerable—lay Optimus Prime's motionless form.

"Go, go, go!" Lennox ordered, and the four of them broke out from behind the pillars and sprinted for cover.

Halfway to safety, Sam veered off and dashed toward Optimus Prime. Behind him, Mikaela screamed, "Sam!" But he didn't hear her. He just knew he had to make it to Prime's side. An enormous pulse blast flung Sam's body into the air as if he were a rag doll. Mikaela's screams sounded very far away as he hit the ground. He lay still. Beside him, the black sand poured out onto the ground and disappeared on the wind.

The next thing Sam knew, he found himself . . . somewhere *else*. Someplace empty, and white, and infinite.

He turned in place, squinting. "Am I . . . am I dead?"

"No, Sam," said a voice from behind him. Sam whirled and saw one of the original Primes—just like in the hologram that Jetfire had shown them. Another Prime flickered into view beside the first, and then another, and another, until eleven Cybertronians surrounded him.

The first Prime spoke. "We are the Dynasty of Primes. We have been watching you. For a long time."

Another Prime said, "You do not yet know the full truth of your past. Nor of your future."

Sam gulped. "I . . . I don't understand. . . ."

A third Prime nodded his head. "You will."

Sam turned, looking at each Prime around the circle as they spoke in turn.

"You have fought for a Prime: our lone descendant. Faced death for one another."

"Together, you are strong. Together, you will realize your destinies."

"For your sacrifice, your courage . . . the Matrix of Leadership is yours."

• • •

Slowly the vast, infinite white receded, and Sam realized he was lying on the ground with Mikaela's arms around him.

Her tears dropped onto his cheeks. "I love you, Sam," she whispered. "Please come back to me."

Sam blinked. He breathed and said, "I love you."

Mikaela froze, her tear-filled eyes widening, and then she crushed Sam to her, laughing and crying at the same time. Black dust particles rose from the ground and whirled, taking the shape of a spike of metal—a dagger with a crystal glowing in its center.

Mikaela and Sam both stared, awestruck, as the Matrix dropped into Sam's hand. He looked into Mikaela's eyes.

"I have to do this," he said.

She nodded and helped him up. "Go. *Go.*"

Sam ran full tilt for Optimus Prime, climbed onto his chest, and plunged the Matrix into Prime's body, like King Arthur returning Excalibur to the stone.

Crackles of electricity crawled over them both as all of the knowledge Sam had stored—all of the history of the entire Cybertronian race—flowed from Sam into Prime. The spark in Prime's chest flared, glowing a brilliant blue, and Prime groaned. "Sam?"

Sam jumped off as Prime rolled over, trying to get to his feet. "I knew there was greatness in you, Sam," Prime said, his voice weak.

"I'm sorry I didn't listen."

Prime's blue eyes looked into Sam's. "But you *did*."

Before Sam could say anything else, the air itself split open and The Fallen materialized right in front of them.

"So very many centuries." The Fallen sneered. "And your worthless race remains the same." A roar exploded from The Fallen's mouth as the Matrix flew into his hand. Another wave of that hand, and an invisible force field slammed Optimus Prime back into the dirt.

"Revenge is mine," The Fallen said, clutching the Matrix. "And now I claim your sun." The air split again, and The Fallen vanished—only to reappear atop the pyramid, two miles away.

"He's gonna turn on the machine!" Sam cried.

"I . . ." Prime tried to rise again. "I don't have the energy."

But then the sound of a wheezing, backfiring engine grew suddenly loud above them—and Jetfire landed. The ancient Transformer wobbled and fell to his knees. "Optimus . . . you are the last of the Primes. You possess powers beyond your own imagining. Take my wings, my engines . . . fulfill your destiny." He coughed up a shower of sparks. "All my life as a Decepticon, I never did a thing worth doing . . . till now."

With a final wheeze, Jetfire slumped into a deep sleep, his energy spent.

Ratchet approached. Prime looked up at him. "Jetfire has made a noble gesture. Let's not waste it."

"Everyone stand back!" Ratchet said, cracking his knuckles. "I'm about to do what I do best!"

Sam and Mikaela got out of the way as Ratchet,

Prime, and Jetfire all disappeared behind a cloud of dust and magnetic discharges. When the dust cleared, Optimus Prime stood, outfitted with wings and powerful, upgraded jet engines: a flying battle machine.

With a sonic boom, he blasted off toward the pyramid.

PYRAMIDS OF GIZA

Simmons kept climbing the pyramid, even as Devastator continued destroying it. From his hiding place, Leo watched Simmons go, and whispered, "Whoa . . . he *is* the Robo-Warrior. . . ."

Inside the pyramid sat the huge sun-harvester machine, ready to be activated, with the Matrix slotted into its base like a key. The Fallen towered next to it, and both Megatron and Starscream stood behind him. Ready.

Outside, Devastator saw Optimus Prime flying toward the pyramid and turned to face him. Right below him, Simmons screamed into his radio: *"Now!"*

From far out on the sea came a single blinding flash as the battleship's rail gun fired. The super-speed steel slug caught Devastator squarely in the chest, and the impact was so immense that it literally shook him apart. The individual construction vehicles rained down around the triumphant Simmons like cast-off toys. Through this carnage, Optimus Prime roared into the pyramid, angling down toward The Fallen just as the sun harvester fired a beam of white light straight up.

But Prime smashed into the top of the tower with the force of a runaway freight train, and the white beam split, splintered, and cascaded around the pyramid's interior, burning holes in Megatron, Starscream, and The Fallen.

"You dare challenge me?" The Fallen bellowed. "I am a Prime!" He swept his hand toward Optimus, gathering his invisible force field to bend gravity and slam the Autobot away. But Prime held up his own hand, and a shimmering shield of energy blocked The Fallen's effects.

"You abandoned that name when you turned on your brothers," Prime growled. "There's only *one* Prime now . . . and my ancestry will be avenged."

As Megatron and Starscream fled, Prime picked up pieces of the broken sun harvester and slammed them into The Fallen, again and again. The force of his blows grew greater with each strike, until The Fallen flung one hand out and opened a wormhole in the air, trying to escape.

But Prime grabbed him, smashed him into the ground, and pulled the Matrix out of its place at the base of the huge machine.

"Wh-what are you going to do?" The Fallen asked, afraid for the first time in his existence.

"Send you somewhere else." The power of the Matrix flared, closing the wormhole that The Fallen had generated and opening up a new one. "A place where no one will hear from you." Prime wrenched The Fallen into the air and looked him dead in the eye. "Ever again."

And he hurled The Fallen into the new wormhole, which closed with a final, sizzling flash.

Outside, the Decepticons had fled; those who remained in the fight had broken ranks when they saw Megatron and Starscream retreating from the pyramid.

Lennox and Epps joined Sam and Mikaela in the aftermath, and the four of them watched as the Twins carried Simmons and Leo—both of them filthy and exhausted, but happy—back from the pyramids.

Mikaela leaned close and whispered in Sam's ear: "Took *all this* . . . to tell me you love me."

Sam couldn't repress a smirk. "You said it first."

She punched his arm. "Only 'cause I thought you were *dead*."

Sam pulled her to him and kissed her as Prime landed nearby—and then his eyes widened in joy as he saw Ron and Judy running toward him.

"Oh, yeah," Lennox said. "Meant to mention that. We found them inside a Decepticon over on the other side of town."

Sam's parents hugged their son, and then hugged Mikaela, and then hugged them both together.

Around their feet, Wheels drove in circles, making little noises that sounded like "Yippee!"